Elver the Eel

The Life of a Camden Harbor Glass Eel

ROCKPORT
MAINE

About the Author

Before internet, cellphones, social media and computers, Jareth Bramblewick grew up wandering the piney woods and creeks of North Florida, where quiet afternoons and curious creatures first sparked his imagination. Eventually, his journey carried him far from the warm, wild backcountry to the rocky coast of Camden, Maine, a place that stole his heart with its salty sea breeze, mossy forests, and working harbor boats.

In Camden, Jareth found a rhythm of life that echoed with wonder. He explored the whispering waters of the Megunticook River, played ice golf across Chickawaukie Pond, and rode the ferry from Rockland to North Haven and Vinalhaven, where spruce-scented air met the open sea. It was here, along Maine's misty shores and shadowed woodland paths, that his love for nature deepened and bloomed into story.

Today, Jareth Bramblewick writes imaginative tales for children and adults of all ages, weaving together the magic of the natural world with the quiet courage of characters who journey through it. His books carry the scent of briny winds and forest rain, and his words invite young readers to look closer, listen longer, and believe in the wild beauty of the world.

2025 Jareth Bramblewick
United States of America
IBSN 979-8-9991260-0-9
Library of Congress Control Number: 2025912166

Megunticook Lake viewed from
a nearby mountain

Want to see where Elver the eel lives in Camden Maine?

Chapter 1
The Call of the Current

Far, far away in the middle of the Atlantic Ocean, there is a mysterious place called the Sargasso Sea. The water is warm and full of floating seaweed. It's quiet. It's deep. It's where Elver the eel was born.

Elver was tiny, almost see-through! Just a few millimeters long, he looked like a wiggly ribbon. He was called a leptocephalus, which means "leaf head." He didn't know much yet, but he knew one thing, the ocean was huge, and he was meant to go somewhere special.

Thousands of baby eels just like him floated beside him. The ocean current gently pushed them along like a slow, peaceful river. They drifted together, day and night, sleeping when they could and dreaming about the world ahead. "Where are we going?" asked one eel. "North!" said another. "To a place called Camden Harbor." "Camden?" Elver repeated. He liked the sound of that. The older eels, just a few days older, told stories. They said Camden was near the land of humans. It had rivers with cold, clear water, soft mossy stones, and tiny bugs to eat. They said there was a river called the Megunticook that flowed through forests and past birds and bears and beavers. "Is it safe?" asked Elver. "Sometimes," said one of the older eels. "But it's where we grow up. It's our destiny." That word, destiny, felt big. Elver liked it.

Every day, the water around them changed a little. It grew cooler. It smelled different. Elver's body changed too. He grew longer, stronger, and his head began to look more like an eel. Soon, he wasn't a leaf anymore. He was becoming something new.

One morning, a bright light came from above. Elver swam toward it and saw something amazing, sunlight shining through blue water. The ocean was getting shallower. "Land must be near!" he said. His friends gathered close. "Do you think this is it?" Elver nodded. "I think we're almost there." They didn't know what Camden would be like. They didn't know what a harbor was. But Elver's heart felt full. He was ready. The journey was just beginning.

CAMDEN
HARBOR

Chapter 2
Land in Sight

The ocean waves gently rocked Elver and his friends. The water was changing. It wasn't as salty now. It was cooler. It smelled… different, like trees and rocks and something fresh. "Do you smell that?" Elver asked. One of his friends named Ripple smiled. "That's land," she said. "We're getting close!"

Excitement rushed through the group. After drifting for almost two years, they were finally arriving at a place they had only heard about in stories, Camden Harbor.

Elver looked around. He wasn't tiny anymore. None of them were. Now they were called glass eels. Their bodies were longer, about the size of a pencil. They were still see through, like living pieces of glass, which is how they got their new name.

"Look at us!" Ripple laughed. "We made it this far. Just like our ancestors." Elver grinned. He was proud. But deep inside, he was also nervous. "Do you think the freshwater will feel strange?" he asked. "Maybe," said another eel. "We've only ever known saltwater." "And what about this thing called a dam?" asked Elver. "What is that?"

Nobody had an answer. The older eels who told the stories never explained what a dam really was. They just said, "You'll know it when you see it." Suddenly, the ground below them rose up. They weren't in the deep sea anymore. Rocks, sand, and seaweed filled the water. And ahead of them, the light changed. It shimmered and sparkled in ways they had never seen before. Elver peeked above the waterline. Boats. Docks. Seagulls. People. It was the human world. "This must be Camden Harbor," Elver whispered.

Before they could say anything more, a dark shape moved above them, fast.

SPLASH!

A giant net came crashing into the water. Elver and his friends panicked. Some swam in circles. Others tried to dive. The net swirled and scooped, and eels were lifted out of the water, gone.

"Ripple!" Elver cried. "I'm okay!" she shouted, dodging the edge of the net. "Keep swimming!" "Where are they taking our friends?" yelled a young eel. "They're called humans," Elver said. "I've heard of them. But I don't know why they're doing this."

The water calmed again. The net was gone, but so were many of their group. Elver's heart ached. "They didn't get all of us," Ripple said, floating beside him. "We still have each other. And we still have our journey." Elver took a deep breath. He looked toward the sound of rushing water coming from the mouth of the river. "That must be it," he said. "The Megunticook River." Ripple nodded. "Then let's go." With strong flicks of their tails, the remaining glass eels swam together. Toward the rushing sound. Toward the unknown. Toward their new home.

Chapter 3
The Wall

The water turned colder and faster as Elver and his friends swam into the Megunticook River. It tasted different, not salty like the ocean, but fresh and clean. It felt tingly on their skin. "We're really here," said Elver. "This is the river from the stories!" Trees leaned over the water. Sunlight sparkled through their leaves. Birds flew above, calling to one another. Pebbles lined the river bottom, and little bugs danced on the surface. It was beautiful.

The glass eels were full of energy and joy. They laughed and darted through the ripples, flipping their shiny bodies like silver ribbons. "I feel like I could swim forever!" said Ripple, spinning in a circle. But the happy feeling didn't last long.

As they swam farther upstream, the sound of rushing water grew louder, much louder. And then, all at once, the river seemed to stop. In front of them was a huge, gray wall. It stretched across the entire river from one side to the other. The water crashed and sprayed where it spilled over the top. The glass eels stopped swimming. "Whoa," whispered Elver. "Is this… the dam?" "It has to be," said Ripple, eyes wide. They had heard the word before, but seeing it now was something else. It was big, and it blocked the way forward. "Why would anyone build a wall in a river?" another eel asked. "I don't know," said Elver. "But it's in our way."

The group floated in silence. The current pushed gently against them, but the wall didn't move. "Can we swim over it?" asked one. "No," said Ripple, "the top is too high." "Can we go under it?" Elver shook his head. "I don't think so. The bottom is solid stone." They all looked at each other. For a moment, no one knew what to do.

Then Elver took a deep breath and swam to the side. He searched the edges of the dam, looking closely. "Hey!" he called out. "Over here! There's a crack!" The others swam over quickly. Sure enough, between some rocks and the concrete, there was a small crevice where water trickled through. "It's not much," said Elver, "but it's something."

CAMDEN

One by one, the eels squeezed through the narrow space. They wiggled, twisted, and climbed with all their strength. It was hard. It was scary. But they didn't stop.

"We're almost there!" someone called out. And then, splash! They popped out on the other side of the wall. "We did it!" shouted Ripple. "We made it over the dam!"

Cheers echoed through the water. The eels spun and danced in celebration. They had faced the wall, and they had won.

Elver looked upstream. The water was calm again. The river curved gently toward the mountains. He smiled. "Let's keep going," he said. "Our home is still waiting."

Together, they swam forward into the next part of their journey.

Chapter 4
Over the Wall

The river above the dam was calm and cool. It felt like a reward after the hard climb. The glass eels swam slowly now, their bodies tired but happy. "We really did it," said Ripple, still catching her breath. "We got over the dam! I thought we'd be stuck there forever," said one of the smaller eels. Elver floated beside them, proud and full of hope. "This is what we're meant to do," he said. "It's what our ancestors did for millions of years. It's in our blood."

As they moved farther upstream, the river changed. The current slowed down. The water grew deeper and wider. They swam past rocks covered in moss, schools of tiny fish, and long leafy plants swaying in the water. "It's so quiet up here," whispered Ripple. Elver looked around. "We must be getting close to the lake." The group swam a little faster now. The water was warmer, and there was more food. Tiny bugs, plant bits, and floating creatures filled the water. The young eels stopped to eat, their energy returning. Suddenly, the river opened up wide, very wide.

In front of them was a huge body of water surrounded by green trees, tall hills, and blue sky. The sun sparkled across the surface like diamonds. Elver's eyes grew wide. "This is it," he said. "This is Megunticook Lake." The eels all gasped. "It's beautiful!" said Ripple. "We made it!" shouted another. "We really made it!" The eels twirled and flipped with joy. They darted between rocks, wove through reeds, and explored every corner of the lake. It was safe. It was peaceful. It was home.

Elver took a moment to look around. He thought about how far they had come, drifting from the Sargasso Sea, escaping the nets, climbing the dam. They had survived it all. And now, they had everything they needed to grow strong. "We'll stay here," said Elver. "We'll eat, rest, and grow." "For how long?" asked one of the younger eels. Elver smiled. "For years. Maybe even twenty." The eels floated together, side by side. They didn't know exactly what the future held, but for now, they were safe, happy, and home at last.

Overlooking Megunticook Lake

Chapter 5
Years of the Lake

Time moved slowly in Megunticook Lake. The seasons changed, but the eels stayed. Elver and his friends no longer looked like glass. Their once see-through bodies had turned darker and stronger. Their muscles grew. Their eyes became wide and golden. They were becoming adult eels, sleek, powerful, and wise.

Spring brought new plants and bugs. Summer made the lake warm and full of life. In the fall, the leaves above the water turned red and orange, floating down like confetti. Winter made the water cold and still, but the eels stayed safe near the muddy bottom, resting together in silence.

Years passed like gentle waves. Elver loved to explore. He knew every rock, every plant, and every hidden spot in the lake. He raced minnows, followed snapping turtles, and once even swam under a family of ducks paddling above him.

Ripple stayed close too. She had grown into a strong and graceful eel. "We've lived here so long," she said one day. "I barely remember the sea." "I remember a little," said Elver. "It was big. It smelled like salt. And it had magic." The other eels nodded. Some remembered the long drift from the Sargasso Sea. Others had only remembered the stories.

As the years went by, something began to change. It started as a feeling, a soft pull, deep in their bellies. A whisper, like a voice from far away. "Do you feel that?" Ripple asked one night. Elver nodded. "Yes. It's like… the lake is telling us it's time." "To go?" Ripple asked. "To leave?" "Yes," said Elver. "Back to the sea." The others felt it too. A gentle ache in their hearts. A longing for something far away. "But this is our home," said one eel. Elver looked around the lake, the water he loved, the rocks he knew, the memories he made. "It is," he said softly. "But we have another home too." Ripple swam beside him. "The Sargasso Sea." Elver nodded. "It's time to go back. It's time to begin the journey… just like our parents did, and their parents before them."

The eels gathered. Some were nervous. Some were excited. But none of them wanted to ignore the call they all felt deep inside.

Together, led by Elver, the eels began to move again, downstream, toward the river, toward Camden Harbor, toward the open sea.

The lake had been good to them. It had helped them grow. But now, the lake gently let them go.

Their journey was not over.

It was only beginning again.

THE SARGASSO SEA

Chapter 6
Downstream Farewell

The water felt different now. The adult eels moved with purpose, gliding through the lake they had known for so long. But this time, they weren't stopping. They were going home, back to the sea. Elver led the way, swimming strong and steady. Ripple followed close behind, and dozens of others formed a long, graceful line, like a silent river within the river. They passed the places they used to play. "Remember that log?" said Ripple, smiling. "We used to hide there." "And that rock!" said another. "That's where we raced the baby fish!" The memories floated around them like bubbles. But none of them turned back. The pull of the sea was too strong.

As they left the lake and entered the Megunticook River, the current helped push them along. It was faster now. Colder. They let the flow carry them, twisting and turning between rocks, under branches, through narrow places they barely remembered from long ago. "It's easier going downstream," said Ripple. Elver nodded. "But it still hurts to say goodbye."

The trees leaned over the river, as if watching them go. Birds called out from the shore. Even the wind felt like it was whispering, "Good luck." Then came the dam. Elver stopped swimming. The others gathered behind him. "There it is," he said quietly. "Still here." "It looks different from this side," said Ripple. They floated for a moment, staring at the giant wall. But this time, they didn't panic. They were no longer small and unsure. They were strong. They were ready. And the dam had slightly changed, too. A narrow channel now ran along one side. It wasn't big, but it was enough, a fish ladder, made by humans to help creatures like them return to the sea. Elver smiled. "Someone was thinking of us." One by one, the eels slithered into the ladder. It was a tight, winding path, but it worked. They slid, swam, and glided down each little step until they popped out into the river below.

They had made it past the dam again. The water smelled saltier now. The pull of the ocean was stronger than ever. They passed the place where the nets had once come down years ago. Elver paused and looked around and smiled. Ripple swam beside him. "But we're still here. And we're almost home."

The water grew deeper, wider, and darker. Boats floated on the surface. Seagulls cried overhead. Then, at last, the river opened into the Camden Harbor.

Elver felt the tide pulling him forward. He looked behind at the river, at the land that had raised him.

"Goodbye, Megunticook," he whispered. "Thank you for everything."
Ripple touched his side with her tail. "Time to follow the sunrise."

And together, they swam out of the harbor, toward the rising sun, toward the open sea.

Life Cycle of the Yellow Eel

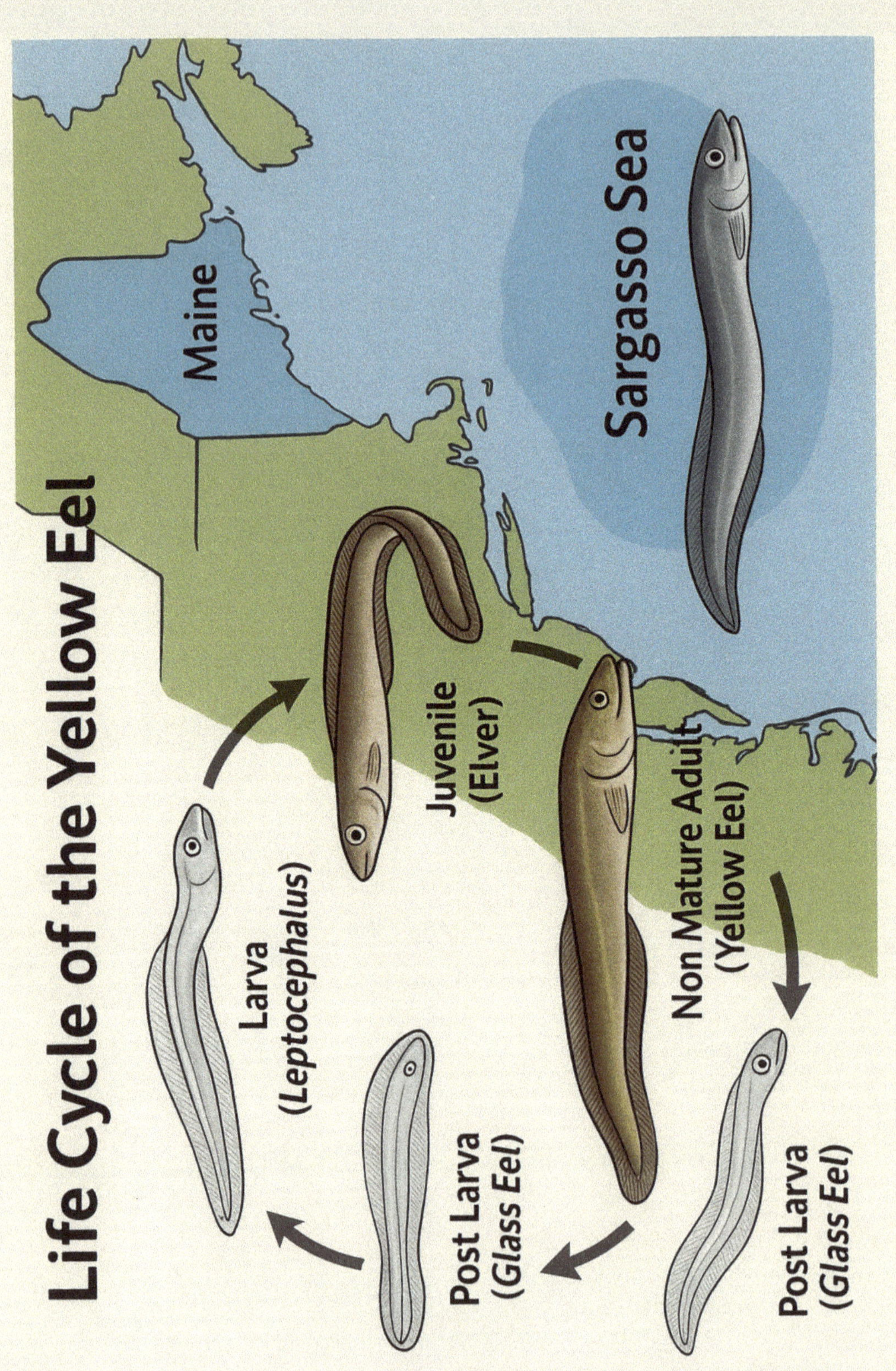

Chapter 7
Return to the Sea

The ocean stretched out in front of them, wide, blue, and endless. Elver felt a deep joy in his heart. He was home… almost. The Sargasso Sea still waited far away, but the salty water, the rolling waves, and the sound of the sea welcomed him like an old friend. The other eels swam beside him, strong and silent, moving as one. "This feels right," said Ripple. "Like we were born to come back." Elver nodded. "We were." They swam deeper into the Atlantic, letting the ocean's currents guide them just as they had when they were tiny and new. The same invisible roads that had brought them to Camden were now pulling them back to where it all began.

Days turned into weeks. The sky above changed with the sun, the moon, and the stars. Sometimes the water was rough. Sometimes it was calm. But the eels never stopped swimming. They passed whales, schools of fish, jellyfish that glowed, and strange glowing creatures deep below. But the eels stayed focused. "Do you remember this part?" one asked. "A little," said Elver. "It's like a dream I had a long time ago."

At last, one early morning, as the sky turned soft with sunrise, the water around them became warmer, thicker, and full of floating golden seaweed. Ripple gasped. "Is this it?" Elver looked around. "Yes. This is the Sargasso Sea." The water swirled gently in all directions. It was quiet. Peaceful. The same magical place where they had been born so many years ago.

The eels slowed their swimming. They circled together, like a spiral, drifting as they once had, only now, they were not babies. They were adults, and they had returned to complete the great journey. Here, in the heart of the sea, life would begin again. New baby eels, tiny, see-through, leaf-shaped leptocephali, would be born. They would float in the same currents, wonder the same thoughts, and dream the same dreams of distant rivers and the land called Camden. Elver closed his eyes and let the ocean rock him. He had traveled far, seen much, and led his friends with courage. Now it was time for the next generation to begin their own adventure. And just like that, the cycle continued.

HARBOR MASTER

Epilogue
The Journey Lives On

Long after Elver and his friends returned to the Sargasso Sea, the ocean still whispered their story.

Some say, if you listen closely near the shore in Camden Harbor, you can hear the gentle swish of eels moving through the water. Some say the river remembers their struggle over the dam, their joy in the lake, and their return to the sea.

In the springtime, when the ocean currents are just right, tiny new eels begin to appear. They drift like leaves in the water, their bodies soft and clear. Just like Elver once was.

They don't know it yet, but they are headed on the same long journey, toward freshwater, toward forests, toward a life full of wonder and change. And maybe, just maybe, one of them will become a leader, just like Elver.

The cycle never ends. It continues, year after year, generation after generation. From the Sargasso Sea, to Camden, to the Megunticook River, and back again. Nature always finds a way. And Elver's journey will always be part of it.

Explore more stories by
J. Bramblewick on Amazon, and dive
into the real life settings with videos
linked through QR codes found
throughout the books.

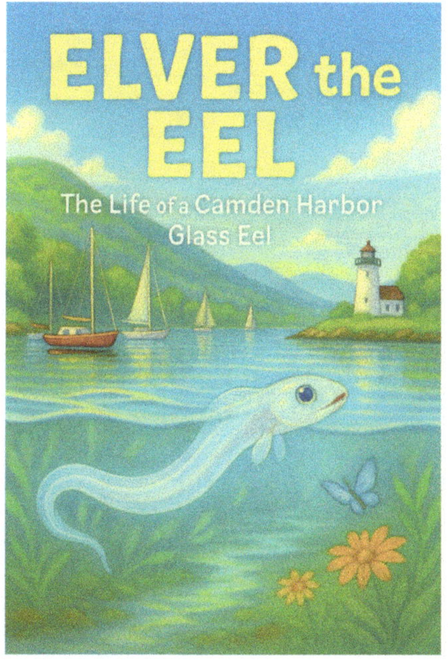

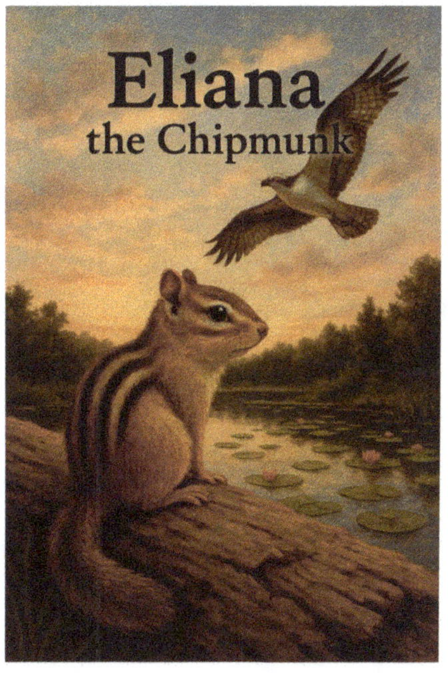

...more adventures and books to
come in the future.

Camden
Harbor

Camden, Maine
A Summer Evening in Another Time

I've wandered through America like a curious breeze, Oregon's pine draped valleys, Wyoming's wide open silence, the sun baked sprawl of Texas, the red-dusted hush of New Mexico. Florida's a humid symphony of whirring machines, and North Carolina hums a similar tune. And everywhere in summer, everywhere, there's the same mechanical chorus, the droning, huffing, hiccupping hum of air conditioners fighting to keep the walls cool and the people sane.

But Camden, Maine? Camden is…different.

I arrived here in November, just in time to be slapped in the face by a winter that laughs at gloves and sneers at snow tires. I endured, I thawed, and now here we are three days after the Solstice and it's a scorcher by Maine standards, low to mid 90s, the air thick enough to drink.

And yet, as I take my evening walk, not a single compressor coughs or groans. No ACs gasping for breath. No mechanical battle cries against the sun. Just open windows. The clink of dishes. The gentle breeze carries the sweet perfume of lilacs, honeysuckle and beach roses. The rhythmic percussion of spatulas and knives. Laughter from the dinner table, soft conversations drifting out like porchlight fireflies.

A grandfather nods from a rocker. A grandmother waves beside him, her eyes kind and knowing. The sun bows low over Camden Harbor, and the air, still warm, wraps around me like an old cotton quilt, not suffocating, just familiar. It feels less like walking through a neighborhood and more like stepping through a time portal. Back to a quieter America, where people didn't need so many machines to feel okay. No compressors. Just community. Just summer. And maybe that's the coolest thing of all.

A true Jewel of the Coast.

Elver the Eel
in Camden Harbor

Elver the Eel
in Megunticook Lake

About the Pictures

Every picture in this book started as a real photo or drawing made by the author. To make them extra fun and colorful, some were turned into cartoon style images using computer tools that help artists, called AI. The pictures are still based on the author's original work, just with a little techy magic added!